To My Beloved Teacher

An anthology of best memories

Anu Lal
Ashwin Ramesh
Rachael Savina Goveas
Mridusmita Das
Dr. Nina Apra
Angel Mary
Eshita Singh
Rajeev A. Masih
Banasmita Das
Kirti V

WRITERS' KALAM
WRITERSKALAM.COM

Title : To My beloved Teacher
Authors : Anu Lal, Ashwin Ramesh, Rachael Savina Goveas, Mridusmita Das, Dr. Nina Apra, Angel Mary, Eshita Singh, Rajeev A. Masih, Banasmita Das, Kirti V

Published by : Writers' Kalam Publishing
Cover Design : Writers' Kalam Studio
Edition Details: I Edition
ISBN : 978-93-343-5188-0

To Kreupasanam, Our Lady of Grace

Contents

Preface

Teachers are those wonderful human beings who help us understand: the world, life, everything. *To My beloved Teacher* is a tribute to all those individuals who took up the role of mentors, teachers, guides and supervisors in our lives. There could be many ways in which one can honour a teacher. To say 'thank you' and to express deep-felt gratitude through literary expression is the best way.

This anthology becomes truly special for us because of its story of perseverance. If this anthology could write an autobiography of a book, it would carry the theme of meeting impossible odds and final survival. Two years ago, in September 2023, when the idea for this anthology was first conceived, I wasn't aware that it would take the whole team of Writers' Kalam Publishing two years to finally publish this book. It took two years and a serious reworking of the initial cover design to prepare the final version of this anthology. Incidentally, this book is the longest anthology project I have ever been part of. With the new cover and the evergreen theme, this book is also one of my favourite anthology projects.

The first submission came in the first month of the 'call for submissions'. Before the next one, we had to wait a whole year. I didn't have the courage to call off the project. We already had one unsuccessful project at hand: an anthology with writings about Delhi, which was part of the 'Colours of India' series. The failure was the aftermath of the drying up of the submission stream with many writers showing interest but not many sharing their works. Consequently, the fear of failure loomed on the horizon for us. As a small publishing house, we don't have a large fund to spend on advertising. So whatever we could do through social media was the only form of advertisement we had.

The next year, we tried again. This time, we expected more engagement as we targeted college students, mostly. However, we were disappointed again, as the call for submissions was answered by just one writer. Thus, a second time, our efforts came to a total disappointment.

The only way forward for this anthology, which we at the publishing house called "the teacher anthology", was oblivion, we thought. Conveying the possibility of shelving the project to the two contributing writers was heartbreaking. So we kept on. And it felt like a lone candle burning in a raging storm, flickering and about to go out at any moment.

Then came 2025. Again, we called for submissions; this time, it was the final call. We made a decision that if we didn't receive enough responses required for a decently sized book, we would just break the sad news to the writers who had already submitted, and close this project down.

Finally, unlike the previous calls, the final one was answered. We started receiving new submissions, and soon it became clear that the book is certainly possible. That's how *To My beloved Teacher* became possible.

A very important lesson learned from this experience is that although in India we have many new writers coming out with books almost every day, there is a considerably low interest in group literary activities. This is mostly due to three reasons.

The first concern is copyright. Writers worry that if they publish their work in anthologies, the particular work would get tied up in the copyright tangle of the anthology, and as a result, they would never be able to use it again without the written consent of the publisher or the compiler of the anthology. Although this is true in many cases, here at Writers' Kalam Publishing, we make sure that we never claim the copyright of the work we publish.

We merely seek the permission to publish a particular work from the writer and revert the full rights of the work to the respective writer. The second concern writers have, which prevents them from entering anthology submissions, is the fear of losing the "unpublished" tag of their work.

Certainly, if the work is released in the public domain, it moves from the “unpublished” to the "published" category. Some writers are too concerned about bagging future publishing contracts that they hesitate to make a commitment to a specific anthology. Most of the publishing houses accept unpublished works and therefore, in the race to get published in a better platform or market, the writer feels insecure in ‘throwing away’ the “unpublished” tag of his or her work for anthologies.

However, in reality, the journey to get published traditionally and successfully is a long one. Anthologies are an important part of the journey because they provide the writer with a reader base. The more anthologies that a writer submits to, the more readers get to know his or her name and nature of work. These readers provide the base and launch pad for the future writer with each new original project. It’s only a matter of time before one of your best works will be recognised by them. Soon, instead of searching for readers, the readers will start searching for you.

The third reason concerns college students, who never responded to the call for submissions. Literary expression seems to be a daunting task for many young individuals now. Instead, they prefer video or audio modes of expression. To use language in written form to create a scene or to communicate an emotion or a thought seems to be a uniquely gifted process.

As a writer with more than a dozen books in my career, I'd like to say what a great joy it is to be a part of this wonderful collection. I'd like to express gratitude on behalf of Writers' Kalam Publishing to each of the writers. As for my readers, I would say that each writer in this anthology has a unique voice. You will enjoy this book as much as we at Writers' Kalam Publishing enjoyed compiling it.

ANU LAL

15 July 2025

Acknowledgments

It is with immense pride and heartfelt gratitude that I extend my sincerest thanks to everyone who made *To My Beloved Teacher* a reality. This anthology has been a long and emotional journey—one marked by challenges, perseverance, and above all, unwavering belief in the power of the written word.

First and foremost, I thank every contributing writer whose voice has added depth and beauty to this collection. Your words are not just stories or tributes—they are bridges between generations, between students and mentors, between memory and gratitude. Your trust in us means everything.

I am profoundly thankful to our Founder Mr Anu Lal whose vision and determination kept this project alive even when hope was dim. His resilience is the backbone of this anthology.

To our editorial and design teams—your quiet strength, late hours, and careful attention to detail brought this book to life. Special thanks to the cover design team for creating a visual identity that truly reflects the spirit of this work.

A heartfelt thank you to our readers and supporters. Your encouragement sustains us and inspires us to keep nurturing literary expression in every form.

Lastly, to the teachers—both remembered and present—who inspired this anthology: this book is a tribute to your legacy. You shape the future in silence, one student at a time. We are forever grateful.

Ankush Bharti

Chief Operating Officer
Writers' Kalam Publishing

"So long as we learn it doesn't matter who teaches us, does it?"

E.R. Braithwaite, *To Sir, With Love.*

To My Beloved Teacher

More than a Light

Ashwin Ramesh

A warm breeze glided past my eyes
In the hours early before the mighty
Sun.
Kept me awake the breeze, when the
skies
Above kept shunning the climbers to
run.
Now before my eyes stood the heights I
Must conquer with the might the breeze
Bestowed upon me, the remnants of my
Long-lost memory of a gentle light
source.

Soon I soared above steep walls of snow,
With sturdy grip of harness and axe I
hold.
Beneath the ice and axe did my hands
glow,
In pitch darkness before sunrise in cold.
The veins strong as steel strings could I
see,

But the sight stopped my ascend for a while
To reminisce the breeze that woke me,
With gentle strokes on my face, to climb.

'What was it?' I wondered, 'that embraced
My heart in cold with tender arms of care?'
And soon rose the bearer of all good deed,
The mighty Sun, with the ever radiant rays.
The warmth reminded of a light source of
The past, which glowed relentlessly for me.
They guided me to reach where I stand now
And move beyond terrains conquered by me.

Oh the warm radiant light glowing on me,
You are more than a light, my beloved guru.
You are the veins of steel in my strong limbs,
And the everlasting tint of endurance in

me.
Oh the might akin to the mighty Sun, I bow
Before your legacy with my humble offerings.
You are more than a light, my beloved guru,
For your faith in my unfathomable leap never dies.

About the Author

Ashwin Ramesh is a native of Kannur, Kerala. He is a teaching faculty at an IAS academy and a Post Graduate student.

Over the years, he has published few of his short-stories, articles and poems. Always devouring concoctions of other worldly words, he loves to read uncommon literary endeavours. He spends his leisure time on Jazz music and hits of the 80s Western music.

Teacher Divine

('25 June 2024)

Rachael Savina Goveas

All of You represent countless virtues,
How do I pick the best or choose?
* Always a protector, who did what's best,
Constantly & cautiously put us to the test.
Understanding our weakness,
Moulding our unique strengths.
Showing us the way, desert or tide,
Making us aware of our banal side.
Never were we abandoned,
Though at times we felt lost,
Making it at the right time,
All worries would be tossed.
We desired more, we needed more proof,
Numerous came along, all mere spoofs!
* You took us all into your flock,
Bound us with love, not one lock.
As one amongst us, you showed no pride,

All knowledge & wisdom, you didn't hide.
Right from the start, you lived in hearts,
Though rejected, you fell not in parts.
Gently yet firmly, you walked the way,
Calling all and sundry into the sway.
No tint of falsehood, not a teeny trace,
Did ever fall upon that magnanimous face.
You fed our minds, washed our souls,
Filling all those forsaken empty holes.
Turned water to wine, you aged with grace,
Healed and cleaned us, left no space.
Raised our hopes, restored our forms,
Cast out evils, and calmed our storms.
Although you had haters, all in sight,
You didn't back down, not a single fight.
How others abused you to the core,
It was easy, but you never settled score.
Till the end, we were your priority
From the start, no show of superiority.
Many have come our way; sadly,
Many, I've seen, are lead astray.
* Even after you left, you kept us strong,
Gifted us a soulful friend before long.
Your teachings through parables
Made complex concepts comprehensible.

When our conscience is put to test,
We recall your words, rise above the rest.
Your humility and love are so divine,
We reach out, trying to be sublime.

About the Author

Rachael Savina Goveas has been teaching since 2010 and enjoys her profession. She likes to observe the wondrous facets of life and transform them into poems and quotes. She has an affinity towards writing 'haikus'. Her poems have been published in the anthologies The Rising Cavalry (Spectrum of Thoughts, 2021), Letters to Life (Humrooh Publication House, 2022), The Equations of Life (Writers' Kalam, 2023) and The Holistic Pine (2023, 2024). Her thoughts are posted on YourQuotes under the name Ray Goveas.

To My Beloved Teacher

Mridusmita Das

Today, the rain drops on the tin roof of my house took me back to my childhood days in Assam. I was lost in the nostalgia of the bygone days. I have been blessed to be born in the valleys where the hearts of the people are filled with love and kindness and Mother Earth blossoms in her full glory.

Suddenly my daughter's voice brought me back to the present. She asked curiously "Ma Kun Tumar favorite teacher" (Mother, who is your favorite teacher?)

I immediately replied, "Geeta Ma'am! You know her!"

"She taught me many life lessons with love and passion. She believed in me when I was clueless. Years passed by but when I met her recently I could still see how she is inspiring thousands of young minds and leading them on their path to success."

My mind tricked me and asked "Do you have only one favourite teacher?"

I started to wonder, "Wasn't I blessed to have so many wonderful people around- my parents, siblings, cousins, teachers, friends - did I not learn so many things from each one of them at different stages of my life?

So could there have been one favourite teacher. I analysed my thoughts and found I learnt through observation and LIFE was my greatest Guru.

Like most of us, my mother was my first teacher who taught lessons of unconditional love and care. I imbibe my empathetic nature from her. Her jovial nature reminds me to smile in hard times even today. Her resilience helped me fight the biggest battles of my life.

My father disciplined me and taught me the benefits and wins of hard work. I used to hate his strict rules as a kid but now as a mother to a beautiful young girl I know how those routines instilled responsibility and accountability in me.

My brother always tested my patience and made me more tolerant to challenges in life. His practical approach to life teaches me skills to survive in adverse situations.

I had the best time with my cousins as a kid. We shared innocent secrets - promised not to tell anyone, discussed everything from our favourite food to books to movies to the girls I hated in school to the first crush and many more.... I now know they knew me so well and they stood by me in the hardest of times. I learnt the art of how to not judge anyone from them.

I asked my daughter, “You know what I learnt from you”. She asked curiously “You learnt from me! What did I teach you Ma?”

"Darling, you teach me each day. I knew I was capable of so many things only after you came into my life. I became fearless to protect you. I discovered my strength because of you. I never knew this side of me ever who could love, care, sacrifice, be strict and enjoy being a child with you once again"

"You know dear Mother Nature taught me many valuable lessons as well. She is the supreme teacher. Nature's ability to adapt to changing environments inspires me to be flexible. Its capacity to heal and recover from adversity like earthquakes, volcanic eruptions, hurricanes teaches us to persevere and be resilient.

The cycles of growth, decay, and renewal that exist in nature for life forms remind us of the importance of letting go and starting anew. The balance and harmony in Nature teaches us to live in sync with the environment and ourselves. Nature's seasons and growth patterns teach us the value of patience and timing.

Diversity and uniqueness of nature inspires us to appreciate and celebrate our differences."

"You know, my little one, if you have the eyes of an observer and the curiosity to learn, you will be able to absorb all the good lessons my greatest Guru LIFE has to offer!"

My daughter smiled and nodded. She hugged and kissed my cheeks and said "I LEARN FROM YOU MAA' (happy tears)

About the Author

She is a project manager with a reputed MNC with over 17 years of IT experience. She is a distinction holder with a 'Bachelor's-In-Engineering' in Electronics and Communication. She has been publishing her poems and write-ups in newspapers and magazines since childhood.

'A WIDOW- REBIRTH FROM HER ASHES' is her debut novel, which was released on 15th August 2023. She shares her journey of self-discovery and transformation in this masterpiece.

Her second venture was a series called 'SPARROWS OF MICHIGAN' which is a fun adventurous read.

She has since then authored 14 best sellers -combining her 5 solo books and 9 anthologies.

Her books in collaboration with Super7 include three bestsellers A QUOTE A DAY MIRACLE EVERYDAY, LOVE CONNECTION, CALM DOWN THE ANGRY BIRD WITHIN: The Mantra to P(e)acify and STORIES OF COURAGE-Vol 1 and 2

Her book BROKEN RELATIONSHIPS -2 FOR TANGO, 3 IS CROWD is a hot favorite amongst her readers.

She recently launched Riya and the Rooster with her 9 year old daughter on 6th March,2025. It is an early learning book for toddlers.

Her 1st poetry collection SYMPHONY- Soulful Rhythm is all set to be released on 21st March 2025 on occasion of World's Poetry Day.

Mridusmita is a prominent speaker. She has been part of Lekhak Manch at the World Book Fair, in 2024.

She spoke for Akashvani- All India Radio Talk Show for North East on World's Women's Day 2024.

She has spoken in various schools and colleges, including IIT Roopar and her Alma mater, Shrimanta Shankar Academy. She has moderated and participated in many author talks.

This young achiever has been covered by 'India Today NE' for her outstanding contribution to literature.

Mridusmita is involved in Charity Work for Street Dogs.

"Sir, You Live On": A Student's Ode to Dr Abdul Qadir

Dr Nina Apra

In the sterile scent of hospital halls,
Where silence meets the beeping calls,
Stood a man of wisdom, calm and grand—
With a healer's mind and a guiding hand.
He was not just the Head we came to know,
But a sculptor of minds, who helped us grow.
His gaze was sharp, his standards high,
Yet kindness always lit his eye.
With a white coat, he wore grace and might,
Turning anxious hours into purposeful light.
He walked through chaos with steady feet,
Making every struggle a moment sweet.

He dreamt of more than skill alone,
He wanted seeds of greatness sown.
Anesthesiologists with the golden touch,
Masters of science, yet hearts as such—
Who felt each pulse, who heard each
sigh,
Who stood for patients, do or die.
He taught us more than drugs and dose,
He taught us how to stay composed.
He built in us a steady core,
Those storms of life could not uproot
anymore.
When illness wrapped me in silent
dread,
Far from my family, confined to a bed—
I, a student, too proud to ask,
He saw through me, took up the task.
He came with words I shall never forget,
"Shall I send my wife to care for you
yet?"
It was not duty, but love so rare,
A father's heart beneath the white he
would wear.
That day, I saw a different side—
Beyond the mentor, love was wide.
In a place of pain and sterile air,
His warmth reminded me that someone
did care.
And then one day, without pretence,

He spoke with warmth and reverence:
"Nina, from you I have learnt anew—
Punctuality, dedication, and the strength to push through."
To hear such words from a teacher revered,
Left my eyes misted, my soul deeply stirred.
Some rewards glitter and fade,
And then there are moments forever engraved.
That single sentence, uttered so true,
It was greater than medals or interviews.
I remember his scoldings, sharp and brief,
Yet filled with purpose, never with grief.
Each correction, each firm stance,
Pushed me to excellence, gave me a chance.
He corrected mistakes not to shame,
But to polish, perfect, and uplift my name.
He believed in me when I had doubts,
Helped my inner voice find its shout.
No longer just my teacher, he remains,
But a timeless presence in my veins.
In every case, I handle with care,
In every act of kindness I dare—
I know he watches, proud and near,

His blessings flow crystal clear.
Though he walks no more these earthly grounds,
His spirit echoes in hospital sounds.
In the rhythm of monitors, the sterile light,
His presence returns each working night.
He lives in discipline, in empathy's name,
In every life touched by his flame.
He lives in the hands that gently hold,
And in stories of strength quietly told.
He is in focus before a spinal prick,
In the patience when the vitals tick.
He is in the silence before a sigh,
In the eyes that refuse to let a patient die.
So I write with reverence and undying aim—
To carry forward his sacred name.
He was more than a mentor, more than a guide,
He was the soul of our academic side.
And I, his student, in awe remain,
Wearing his values, bearing his flame.
His lessons, both clinical and life-long, too,

It has shaped my being, through and through.
May I serve with the grace he gave,
May I remain humble, kind, and brave.
And when I teach, may I also be—
A light, a hope, a legacy—like he was to me.

So this is my tribute, my heartfelt song,
For a man whose guidance made me strong.
With folded hands and tear-brimmed eyes,
I whisper thanks beneath the skies.
Thank you, Sir, for each stern word,
For every lesson deeply heard.
For standing tall when I was weak,
For showing strength, one need not shout, but speak.
You lit a torch in corridors dim,
And helped me rise when hope was slim.
You shaped the doctor I strive to be—
One of the skills, but more of humanity.
Your legacy is not just in what you taught,
But in the compassion you gently brought.
Though you are not here for me to see,
I feel your presence guiding me.

And with each life I strive to save,
I send my thanks from heart to heart.
May the world remember your sacred part—
As a healer, a teacher, and a man of heart.

About the Author

Meet Dr Nina Apra, an unstoppable force of resilience, creativity, and empowerment. A woman of many talents and passions, she has seamlessly woven her life's adversities into her extraordinary achievements, emerging as an award-winning anesthesiologist, bestselling author, dynamic orator, and passionate social activist. Dr. Apra's life is an example of the power of perseverance, and through her multifaceted career, she continues to inspire countless individuals to live fearlessly and embrace their true potential.

Dr Apra's literary journey is nothing short of remarkable. An author of bestselling books such as:

1. ECHOES OF LIFE: UNSCRIPTED TRUE STORIES OF RESILIENCE AND TRIUMPHS

2.SACRED SILENCES: WAR, LOVE, LOSS.

3. HORROR MANGTA KYA

4. STORIES OF COURAGE VOLUME 2

5.BENEATH: MIND MATTERS A book on mental health

6. SCARSCRIPT : A romance fiction

She has captivated readers with her unparalleled storytelling. Her ability to channel deep emotions and personal experiences into her writing sets her apart as a unique voice in contemporary literature.

Dr Nina Apra is far more than an author. She is a multi-faceted artist—a poetess, singer, dancer, and stand-up comedian, blogger, avid storyteller—who radiates joy, humour, and passion, love in all she does. Her charisma and ability to connect with people have made her a beloved personality on stage and off. Whether making audiences laugh with her witty stand-up performances or moving them with her heartfelt poetry, Dr Apra's talents transcend genres and mediums.

She, participated in TED X PCTE LUDHIANA, INDIA, 7th March 2025 as a speaker where she set the stage on Fire by her innovative heartwarming ideas and her compelling true stories of her life and lives she has touched.

Her accolades are as diverse as her talents. Dr Apra has been honoured with prestigious awards such as the Indian

Author Award, the Voice Award, the Change Maker of the Year Award, and the Best Women Employee Award, among many others. Her selfless contributions during the COVID-19 pandemic earned her the COVID Warrior Award, recognizing her dedication and bravery on the front lines. In addition to these honours, she has received numerous accolades for her academic excellence and contributions to social causes, establishing her as a respected figure in the medical community and beyond.

As a certified CPR and COLS trainer, and a POSH (Prevention of Sexual Harassment) trainer, Dr Apra is deeply committed to saving lives and creating safer environments for all. Her advocacy for women's empowerment, mental health, and the dignity of women and children reflects her passion for making a positive impact on society. She continues to use her voice as a social activist to uplift others, serving as a light of hope for those facing their struggles.

Despite her many achievements, Dr Apra's aspirations reach even higher. Through her experiences—from overcoming personal and professional challenges to achieving great success—she hopes to empower others to face their obstacles with strength and determination.

Whether she is writing a gripping horror story, delivering a moving speech, or using her voice to advocate for social change, Dr. Nina Apra is a true change-maker. Her unique blend of talent, heart, and perseverance makes her not just an author or a doctor, but a transformative force in the world—someone who uplifts, inspires, and reminds us all of the power within ourselves to triumph against the odds.

Follow her for more updates on books and more !

https://www.amazon.in/stores/author/B0D5LWLC1Q/about : Amazon author page

https://www.facebook.com/profile.php?id=61560295145925&mibextid=ZbWKwL : Facebook author page https://www.facebook.com/profile.php?id=61558769906592&mibextid=ZbWKwL : facebook account

https://www.instagram.com/drninaapra?igsh=bW45Ympkd3Vibmhl : instagram

https://www.linkedin.com/in/dr-nina-apra-85048185 : linkdin

https://medium.com/@drninaapra

https://english.pratilipi.com/user/nina-apra-h9480idi75?utm_campaign=general&utm_source=web_share

drninaapra9896: you tube channel

Book links : https://mybook.to/pjtB

https://amzn.in/d/2tY3Lk9

https://amzn.in/d/g0m6EJS

https://play.google.com/store/audiobooks/details?pcampaignid=books_inapp_orson_options_share&id=AQAAAEDSzVKNkM

A Path of Light: My Beloved Parents

Angel Mary

My first mentors in the journey of life,
In their words, I found my first lesson,
Where I learned the words of wisdom,
Learned how to be happy and do good things,
My first authors, who shaped me with good thoughts and deeds,
The roots of my strength, wings of my dream,
They protected me with their gentle hands,
Their words bloomed like gentle petals, spelling grace,
With every step I take, their inspiration walk beside me...

About the Author

Angel Mary born in Kasaragod, Kerala is an Assistant Professor of English and a dedicated poet with a deep passion for capturing the beauty of nature and the power of hope through her words. Her poetry reflects a profound connection to the natural world, often exploring themes of renewal, resilience, hope and the quiet strength found in everyday moments. Through her work, Angel strives to inspire readers to find light and hope, even in the darkest of times.

Poetry

My Beloved Teacher and I: A Tribute to Life

Eshita Singh

My best teacher is not a person in a classroom.
It is not someone I see every day.
My best teacher is Life itself.

Life has taught me how to walk through storms.
It has shown me how to rise after I fall.
How to let go of pain.
How to grow beyond fear.
How to leave behind what no longer serves me.

Life has whispered truth in silence.
It has screamed through heartbreak.
It has held my hand in moments of confusion.
And pushed me forward when I was stuck.

It taught me who truly loves me.
And who only wears the mask of love.
It taught me to trust my instincts.
And to understand that not everyone
who smiles is kind.

Life taught me that mistakes are not the
end.
They are new beginnings in disguise.
But only if I accept them.
Only if I take ownership of them.

Life showed me
that it's okay to be imperfect.
That we are all here to learn.
That every person who comes into my
life
has a lesson for me.

Nothing happens without a reason.
Every bird that flies by,
every word spoken,
every heartbreak,
every embrace—
everything has meaning.

Life has introduced me to darkness,
but it also showed me the sunrise.
It gave me nights full of pain,

but also mornings filled with peace.

It has taught me about people—
those who wound,
and those who heal.

Life has shown me the beauty of
forgiveness.
Not for others,
but for my own peace.

It taught me to live in gratitude.
To thank every moment,
even the ones that broke me.
Because they built me too.

Life is not just a path.
It is the teacher walking beside me,
within me,
every second,
shaping me
into who I am meant to be.

And for that,
I will always be grateful.

About the Author

Eshita Singh is a dynamic and passionate author, motivational speaker, banker, and spiritual seeker based in Jaipur, with roots in the culturally rich city of Varanasi. A Branch Manager at the State

Bank of India, she gracefully balances her professional life with her calling as a writer and change maker. Eshita's literary journey gained momentum with the release of her debut novel *Happens Like a Dream* in 2021, a heartfelt fiction love story that gently touches on themes of self-love and personal growth. The book became a bestseller and marked the beginning of a flourishing writing career.

In 2023, she released Redefining Success for Empowered Living, another bestselling work that redefined the concept of success through a body-mind-soul approach, and inspired countless readers to embrace a more fulfilling and authentic life. Her third book, The Art of Effective Parenting (2024), offered heartfelt insights from her personal journey as a mother. The same year, she led a collaborative book titled Love Connection, a collection of short love stories written by seven authors, and Sugar and Brownies, her first poetry collection dedicated to her son, was released in December.

One of her most powerful contributions to literature is *Devi: Flames of*

Empowerment (2024), a book that celebrates the divine feminine within each of us. It emphasizes that empowerment is not bound by caste, creed, or gender—it emerges from pain, transformation, and inner strength. The book sparked meaningful offline engagement through awareness activities and sessions focused on women empowerment. Eshita is currently working on its sequels, which feature the stories of real-life, unsung "she-heroes"—ordinary women with extraordinary strength and resilience. These inspiring narratives aim to create a ripple of hope and courage in society.

Beyond writing, Eshita is a speaker who has delivered impactful talks in schools and colleges across India, focusing on emotional healing, self-awareness, and empowerment.

Rooted in deep values and driven by purpose, Eshita Singh continues to inspire through her words, her actions, and her unwavering belief in the transformative power of stories.

Prose

Teaching and a teacher!

Rajeev A. Masih

A dictionary defines teacher as a person who teaches particularly in a school but whoa! Wait a second and hold your horses.

Why so? Why to hold your horses?

Because practically speaking, the role and profession of a teacher isn't just limited to teaching only; as a teacher is expected to be more like a melodramatic Bollywood hero or a heroine, for that matter, who is multi-talented and carries an unlimited power to tackle all the problems but this is a misconception, about a teacher and as a result the main role of a teacher to teach gets affected severely.

Added to it, is the fact that a teacher, has to deal with 50 students or even more, in a class. And the real problem starts when, in that group of 50 students, 30 are not interested in any subject, at all, but are forced to come to the school by their parents.

Then the challenge to teach the students becomes all the more heavy because those 30 uninterested students create an intentional disturbance.

Moreover, it is a high time when it must be realized by everyone that a teacher is 'a human being' too, with very real difficulties at the backend - like health issues, family problems and financial challenges.

Now here comes the dirty part, which might not be acceptable to many and when talking about the financial challenges, then is the world aware that many teachers working in the private schools are underpaid and the situation is the same, more or less everywhere in maximum public schools?

And YET, in spite of all these problems, difficulties and challenges, a teacher helps in the growth of a country by teaching but instead of being honoured in any way, what we have are the movie stars, the cricket players, the models and the local politicians who are appreciated and respected by the society.

Isn't it disheartening?

Thus before anyone decides to be a teacher, let her / him, be aware and awake of the bitter realities related about teaching and a teacher.

About the Author

Rajeev A. Masih, is a double postgraduate, an M.A. in English and in Sociology, along with with a few other supportive educational achievements.

He is an author by choice and loves to write on various topics and themes.

A proponent of spontaneity, the author can be reached through an email: mshrjm@gmail.com

Instagram Id : @masih.rjm

I Wish

Kirti V

I wish to be that little girl,
Who runs into your arms
Everyday at school.

I wish to be that little girl,
Who waits for you to hold hands,
And walk into the class.

I wish to be that little girl,
Who loves the way you teach,
To write cursive, leaving one-finger gap.

I wish to be that little girl,
Who eagerly waits to be called out,
By you Deena ma'am, my first grade
teacher.

About the Author

Kirti, a teacher by profession and a poet by passion is a multilinguist, a voracious reader and an orator. She has authored three solo poetry books (Tides of Life, From My Pen and Poetic Pearls) and has contributed to around 50+ anthologies. Her works can be read from www.kirtisignature.com and she can be reached at kirti.v@gmail.com

Prose

Equations to Empathy: Chitra Chowdhury's teaching Legacy

Banasmita Das

There are women who live quietly, yet leave behind echoes in every room they once walked. My grandmother, Chitra Chowdhury — to us she is always Junu Pehi — was such a woman. To her students at Tarini Choudhury (TC) Govt. Girls High School, she was Chitra Baidow: a firm mathematics teacher and later the Respected Principal. She was known for her crisp white Mekhela Saadors, strict eyes behind her spectacle, chalk-dusted fingers, precise explanations and a heart full of patience. But to us, her grandchildren, she was our lighthouse — our first storyteller and our silent, constant protector.

I still remember the scent of talcum powder mingling with the pages of her old textbooks and the warm, comforting aroma of freshly baked nankatta which she prepares for us. Her voice — clear and deliberate — held the kind of command that made you not just listen, but truly learn.

A Standard of Excellence

Chitra Baidow was not merely a teacher by profession; she was a teacher by nature. At TC School, where she taught for decades, she was more than an educator — a benchmark of discipline, intellect and unshakeable integrity. Her mathematics classes were never easy, but under her guidance, mathematics transformed from a subject many feared, into a puzzle to be solved — a language to be decoded and enjoyed. Students often say her classes were challenging, but deeply inspiring.

Even today, her former students speak of her with unhidden affection. Many have gone on to become teachers themselves, doctors, professionals or devoted homemakers — each shaped, in some way, by her influence. She touched lives with quiet, lasting grace. Even after retirement, students and colleagues alike would visit her, sending gifts, letters or messages. Some of her students brought their children to meet her, hoping they too could receive a glimmer of the wisdom she had once offered so generously.

The Heart of her Greatest Classroom

But her greatest classroom, I believe, was the home. We, her grandchildren, were perhaps her most devoted students. While she did taught us mathematics, but the most profound lessons were in the way she lived which was never written in any textbook.

She taught us through her actions: the power of selfless love and sacrifice, the quiet dignity of leading a disciplined life on one's own terms, the importance of staying connected to our roots & culture and the simple art of giving without expecting anything in return.

Junu Pehi was a lady who was not loud with her love and affection, but silent, constant and unshakeable. Her way of showing it was through care and concern for every being. Her strength came not from grand gestures, but from the enduring silence of sacrifice — from always putting others before herself without a word of complaint.

Lessons to be learnt from her were everywhere, if you were paying attention.

Her Enduring Presence

Though she is no longer with us, Junu Pehi's teachings are etched into every part of who we are — just like the accolades and honours that still hang proudly on the walls of her room. They remind us not only of her achievements, but of the values she lived by.

Former students continue to reach out to us. Some share how they chose to become educators because of her motivation. That, I believe, is the true legacy of a teacher: not only the knowledge imparted, but the belief planted in uncertain hearts. The quiet transformation of doubt into possibility.

A Legacy beyond Walls

They say great teachers never die — and I believe that with all my heart. I carry her with me still: in the way I envision life and its purpose, in the way I strive to take her legacy forward and in the way I search for meaning in small, quiet things.

Her classroom once had four walls. Now, it stretches across generations — living on in every life she touched, and in every lesson she whispered into the world.

About the Author

Banasmita Das, a passionate writer and poet from Assam, whose work spans travel essays, literary articles, book reviews and Japanese tanka, featured in The Assam Tribune, Booknerdection, Spillwords and Coldmoon journal. She curates her writing on her blog Literary Voyage. Her acclaimed debut poetry collection, Gilded Verse, released in 2025.

About Writers' Kalam Publishing

Writers' Kalam is India's latest knowledge-based education venture where publishing and education go hand-in-hand. It is an ensemble of a few passionate leaders who are industry experts in both education as well as publishing.

Writers' Kalam is a pan-Indian, international space for writers, readers, and students. The purpose of Writers' Kalam is to bridge the chasm that exists amidst literary-artistic-epistemic production for those who are in the margins of opportunities. We envision to open opportunities to at least a hundred writers to get their works published through our various platforms. These opportunities are available for everyone irrespective of caste, creed, or financial background. Our various platforms include: Writers' Kalam Literary Bulletin online and Print (Upcoming), TheHolisticPine.com Online journal, The Holistic Pine Print issue, Tribute Print issue, and our anthologies.

Writers' Kalam is founded by renowned Indian English author Anu Lal.

www.ingramcontent.com/pod-product-compliance
Lightning Source LLC
Chambersburg PA
CBHW050025170726
48282CB00025B/548
9789334351880